The Fourth-Grade Four

THE
Fourth-Grade Four

—○○○○—

MARILYN LEVINSON

Illustrated by
Leslie Bowman

A TRUMPET CLUB SPECIAL EDITION

For Bernie, David, and Michael.
And for children everywhere
who wear glasses.
—M.L.

Published by The Trumpet Club
666 Fifth Avenue, New York, New York 10103

Text copyright © 1989 by Marilyn Levinson
Illustrations copyright © 1989 by Leslie Bowman

ISBN: 0-440-84412-6

This edition published by arrangement
with Henry Holt and Company, Inc.
Printed in the United States of America
October 1991

10 9 8 7 6 5 4 3 2 1
BPR

Contents

1

A Visit to the Doctor

Mrs. Burman parked the car behind the medical building. She turned to Alex. "Here we are, just in time for our appointment."

Alex didn't move. He stared out the window with his arms crossed—the way his father sat when he *knew* he was right but no one agreed with him.

"Let's go, Alexander. The doctor is waiting."

Alex knew that his mother had left her job early so they could see the doctor, but still he didn't move.

"My eyes are fine," he said.

"Mrs. Hennessey doesn't think so." Mrs. Hennessey was the school nurse.

"Mrs. Hennessey doesn't know beans about anything."

Mrs. Burman sighed. "She knows how to give eye tests. And she wasn't happy with yours."

Alex looked down. "Well, maybe she was wrong. I can see just fine."

His mother patted his arm. "We'll let Dr. Coleman decide that, won't we?"

"You're wasting a lot of money for nothing," Alex said. "And the doctor will probably keep us waiting a long time."

"That's okay," his mother said. "You're worth it."

And with that, Alex knew he was sunk. He opened the car door and got out.

The waiting room was empty. A bad sign, Alex thought. That meant the doctor would see him next. And maybe give him the news that would ruin his life.

Alex wished he were with Billy and Steve. Billy and Steve were his best friends. Together they formed Los Tres Amigos, which meant "the three friends" in Spanish.

Alex couldn't help smiling as he remembered how Los Tres Amigos began. It was the Saturday of Labor Day weekend, and he and Steve were sleep-

ing over at Billy's house. They'd spent the afternoon playing softball in the school yard with other
boys. Then, after a barbecue of hot dogs and hamburgers, they'd watched *Three Amigos!* on the VCR.
Billy had come up with the idea of calling them-
selves Los Tres Amigos—like the actors in the film.

"Let's swear a pact of friendship and adventure,"

Alex had shouted. And it was Billy who thought of making milk shakes so they could seal their oath with a drink.

And it all was going great until Billy's dog came into the kitchen and knocked over the blender. Then he lapped most of it up before they had a chance to clean up the mess.

Alex shook his head sadly. Right this very minute his friends were playing ball in the school yard. They weren't sitting around in some dumb office, waiting to have their eyes examined.

Mrs. Burman spoke through the little window to the nurse sitting at her desk. Alex squinted so he could see the nurse's face. Lately he was squinting a lot. It helped him see better. Mrs. Burman answered questions such as where did she and Alex's father work? Did either of them wear glasses? (No, they didn't, so why should I? Alex thought. It wasn't fair.) Then she filled out forms.

Alex sat next to his mother and worried. She had told him that the doctor wouldn't do anything that would hurt, but Alex couldn't be sure. Mothers were supposed to say things like that. Besides, he hated the idea of someone examining his eyes. The very thought made him blink.

"Stop kicking," his mother told him.

"I'm not," Alex answered. But he *was* kicking the back of his seat, so he stopped. He always kicked when he was nervous.

The doctor came out. He was big and bald-headed, about the same age as Alex's grandfather. He wore glasses and a smile, and a white coat over his regular clothes. He came right up to Alex and stuck out his hand for Alex to shake.

"You must be Alex Burman. I'm Dr. Coleman. I'm going to take a look at your eyes. Feel free to look into my eyes while I'm looking at yours."

Dr. Coleman laughed at his own joke. Did he really think it was funny? Alex stared at the brown carpet. Soon Dr. Coleman would know. Then he'd tell Alex's mother, and the whole world would find out—that Alex Burman couldn't see very well. That he probably needed to wear glasses. Every day. For the rest of his life.

The examining room was dark. Alex had to look through a machine, something like a Viewmaster

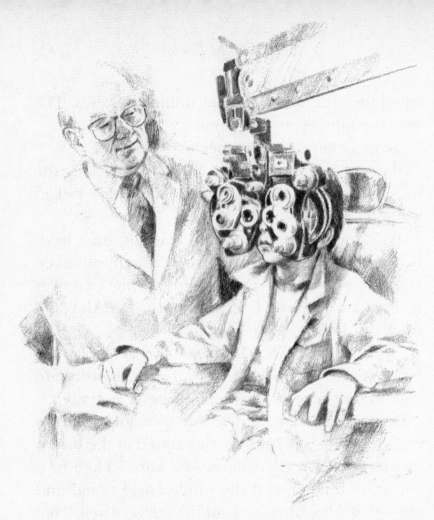

except that it was much bigger and was attached to
a thick pole. The doctor put a black lens over Alex's
left eye so he could see only with his right one.
Then Dr. Coleman started changing lenses.

"Look at the eye chart on the wall and tell me which is better—one or two."

"Two," Alex said, since the letters were clearer the second time. And they kept on getting clearer each time Dr. Coleman switched to a different lens. It was great being able to read all the letters without squinting. Even the tiny, littlest letters on the very last line.

But all this meant something terrible—that Alex could see better through the lenses. Which meant . . . The eye chart was probably the same one as in Mrs. Hennessey's office. Alex realized that he should have gone in during lunchtime and memorized it. Now it was too late.

After Alex chose the lens that made the eye chart the clearest, Dr. Coleman had him do the same with his left eye. Then he had Alex read something with both lenses to make sure he could read the letters. Alex could.

Dr. Coleman didn't stop there. He took a kind of flashlight and peered into Alex's eyes from all angles while Alex stared at different points in the room. He had Alex follow red and green lines through some lenses to see where they met. Finally Dr. Coleman put drops in his eyes and said that everything would turn blurry for a while.

"The nurse will take you back to the waiting room. It takes a few minutes before the drops work."

"But why do I need drops in my eyes?" Alex asked. He didn't want Dr. Coleman to know, but it was scary not to be able to see.

"So I can examine your eyes better. Soon I'll know everything I need to about your eyes."

Alex slumped into the same seat he was sitting in before. He started kicking.

"Are you all right?" his mother asked.

"Yeah," he answered.

But he wasn't all right. He was far from all right. He was going to be the class nerd. The biggest jerk. The only boy in his fourth-grade class who had to wear dumb glasses, if you didn't count Peter Lesser. And Peter Lesser, even though he was the smartest kid in fourth grade, *didn't* count.

It seemed like half a day later when the nurse led Alex back into the examining room.

"Do you feel funny?" the doctor asked as he looked into Alex's eyes.

"Yeah, I can hardly see."

Dr. Coleman gave an understanding chuckle. "It takes a few hours for those drops to wear off. At least you have a perfect excuse not to do your homework tonight. I'll write a note for your teacher when we're finished."

Big deal, Alex thought. It didn't make up for what he knew was coming.

Finally Dr. Coleman finished studying his eyes. He brought Alex into his consultation office and asked the nurse to get Mrs. Burman.

Alex was tired and hungry and grumpy. He rubbed his eyes, wishing he could make the drops disappear.

"Well, young man," Dr. Coleman boomed—as though he were giving Alex the best news in the world—"it looks like you're going to start wearing glasses early in life. You're myopic, which means you can't see well in the distance."

As if I didn't know, Alex thought. Still, it shocked him to hear the doctor say the words out loud. He was secretly hoping that he wouldn't need glasses yet. Alex felt like crying. But he wouldn't. He was one of Los Tres Amigos and a left wing on his all-boys soccer team. He was nine and a half. Almost ten. He almost never cried anymore.

". . . and they have all these modern-style frames," the doctor was saying. "Not like the horrid ones I had to wear as a boy."

"Not to mention prescription sunglasses," Mrs. Burman added. She laughed. "They make you look like a movie star!"

Cripes! The doctor and his mother were talking about his wearing glasses like it was some new style of clothing instead of the worst possible thing that could happen to him! Alex clamped his lips shut. He refused to say another word until he was out of that office.

2

"I Won't Wear Them— *I Won't!*"

Finally Dr. Coleman and Alex's mother finished talking, and Alex was able to go home.

Alex got into the car and scrunched down in his seat. Who ever heard of a soccer player wearing glasses? Alex couldn't imagine wearing glasses to his soccer games on Saturday. They'd only get in the way. And what if the ball should hit the glasses? They'd probably break into little pieces and blind him!

And then there was Billy.

Alex could just imagine what Billy would say if he ever saw glasses sticking out on Alex's face. Billy was the leader of Los Tres Amigos for good reason.

Aside from being a great all-around athlete, Billy was big and strong and not afraid of anything. Alex bet he wouldn't even be afraid to spend a night in a haunted house all by himself. Billy made everything exciting. It was Billy who had found the shack in the woods behind the high school that they sometimes used as a clubhouse. And he had this great way of taking something ordinary and changing it just enough to turn it into an adventure. Like bike riding in the rain. Or camping out in Steve's backyard. And it was Billy who was always on the lookout for anyone who was different. Then he called out what he noticed.

"Hey, Four Eyes!" he sometimes shouted at Peter Lesser. "Do you see two of me?"

"Good morning, Lard Body," he greeted chunky Suzie Williams each day.

Although Alex would never insult anyone like *that*, he and Steve always laughed when Billy did this. To show Billy that they were on his side. After all, they were Los Tres Amigos and had to stick together. Alex shook his head. He sure didn't want to give Billy and Steve reason to laugh at *him*.

"Let's see," Mrs. Burman said as she turned onto Primrose Lane, where they lived. "I have to work late tomorrow, so we can't get your glasses then."

Good, Alex thought. Besides, he had soccer practice tomorrow afternoon.

"I guess we'll have to wait until Friday afternoon," his mother said.

At dinner Alex's mother told his father about their visit to the eye doctor and how the doctor had said he had to get glasses.

Alex hardly listened. He was busy working on a plan. Sure, he'd get the glasses so his mother wouldn't keep on nagging him. But that didn't mean he had to wear them. Alex smiled for the first time that day. I'll get them, but I won't wear them, he thought to himself. Not in a million years.

He wouldn't wear the glasses in school. Or with his friends. Or at soccer games. Only when he was in the house. Alex started gobbling down his spaghetti and hamburgers double-time.

"Hey, slow down, Alex," his father said, "or you'll get a stomachache."

"Sure thing, Dad," he answered, feeling more like himself.

He'd solved his problem by using his head—just like his father always told him to do. Then he remembered the doctor's note, which excused him from doing his homework. Alex smiled again.

3

An Unpleasant Surprise

Alex hurried to school the next morning. It was Thursday, a gym day. For Alex, gym was one of the best things about school—along with recess and being with his friends. Fourth grade was his best year ever. Alex felt important. He was on the soccer traveling team, and he belonged to a group. He was one of Los Tres Amigos.

Alex hadn't known Billy until this summer because they'd never been in the same class. Steve had just moved to the neighborhood. The three of them had become good friends at day camp. Actually, on the very first day. They were on the same softball team and immediately discovered how well they played together. In the second inning Billy pitched a ball that the batter bounced back at him. He fielded it and threw the ball to Alex, the first baseman, and Alex got the ball to Steve at second base in time to tag out the runner for a double play! It was like magic! It felt like they'd been playing ball together for years. When they took their turns at bat, they cheered each other on. Alex, who was always a good athlete, found he played even better with Billy and Steve at his side.

And so the summer went. Even when the counselors insisted on splitting them up because any team the three of them were on almost always won, the special bond between them held. Soon Alex, Steve, and Billy were always together after camp and sleeping over at each other's houses on the weekends. They often rode around on their bicycles, looking for new places to explore. Or they played ball with other kids in the school yard. They went out on Steve's family's boat, and Alex's parents took them to the beach. It was the best summer Alex ever had.

By the time school started, they were Los Tres Amigos. It was fun having Billy and Steve greeting him: "Hey, Amigo!" It was fun being in fourth grade, knowing that next year they would be fifth graders and the oldest in the school. Alex didn't care that Billy, Steve, and he were all in different classes. Just as well, really. This way his friends wouldn't know if he did badly on a test. Or if he got into trouble for not paying attention.

Alex always *tried* to pay attention in class. He listened when his teacher, Mrs. Miller, explained something new in math or in English. But once the class started doing examples, Alex's mind began to travel. It traveled out the classroom window to the soccer field and Alex's next game. Or to some secret place where Los Tres Amigos could build a new clubhouse that no one would ever find—not in a million years. Mrs. Miller said that Alex had to *concentrate* on his schoolwork. Alex agreed, but he couldn't stop his mind from traveling.

Alex got to school just as Billy's bus arrived. Billy was the first one off the bus.

"Hey, Amigo! We missed you yesterday. We had a great soccer game going. Our team would have won if we had you as a forward."

Alex turned red. "I had to go shopping with my mother." He didn't like to lie, but if he told Billy the truth, Billy would laugh.

"Anyway, we'll get a game up at recess. See you, Amigo."

Billy held up the palm of his hand and made a circle as if he were wiping a foggy window. Alex did the same.

"See you at recess," Alex said.

He walked into his classroom, not as happy as he was before he'd seen Billy. Alex wished he didn't have to lie to Billy. He wished Billy understood about things like wearing glasses, instead of laughing at them. That was because there was never anything wrong with Billy. He wasn't afraid of anyone or anything. Alex sighed. Why me? Why did the doctor say *I* have to wear glasses?

The day began like all the others—they said the Pledge of Allegiance. Then Mrs. Miller announced that there was an assembly after lunch. Everyone clapped. It meant no work that afternoon. When the classroom was quiet again, Mrs. Miller said, "Now put all your books on the floor. We're going to have our spelling test."

Today? But today was Thursday. They always had their spelling test on Friday.

"But we can't have it today," Alex said. "It's Thursday."

The class started laughing. Mrs. Miller pointed to the blackboard. "Here it is, Alex. In big capital letters. And I announced it yesterday. Twice. You probably weren't listening."

"But I— I didn't—" Alex began, upset. Maybe he wasn't the smartest kid in his class, but he always did his work. Then he remembered Dr. Coleman's note. He brought it over to Mrs. Miller, who was giving out paper to the first row.

"What is it, Alex?" she asked, annoyed. "We're having the test today and that's that."

"I couldn't study last night," he whispered. "I had to go to the eye doctor, and he put drops in my eyes."

Mrs. Miller read the note. "I'm sorry, Alex," she said, "but you should have studied before you went to the eye doctor. The announcement about the test has been on the board since Monday."

Alex returned to his seat, which was the third in the row next to the windows. When he squinted at the blackboard, he could just make out the words about the spelling test. Alex was upset. How could he have forgotten something important like a spelling test being changed? And Mrs. Miller didn't even care that he had to have drops put in his eyes.

He wrote the heading on his spelling paper and numbered from one to twenty.

"Number one is 'appropriate,' " Mrs. Miller said. "This is an appropriate gift."

Were there two *p*s or three in "appropriate"? Alex wondered. Today sure was starting out badly.

4

Changing Seats

When the spelling test was over, Mrs. Miller said, "It's time to change seats again." Some of the kids groaned. Not Alex. He was glad they were changing seats. Maybe he'd get to sit in the front row and be better able to see the blackboard. Allison Peters and Laurie Doyle rushed up to the front of the room and whispered to Mrs. Miller. Mrs. Miller said out loud, "Sorry, girls. I'll decide who sits where."

The girls returned to their seats, frowning. Alex smiled to himself. At least Mrs. Miller didn't make exceptions for anyone.

"First row," Mrs. Miller announced. "Bobby De-Vito, Jill, Laurie, and Danny." Alex and his classmates gathered up their books. They took their new seats or stood in the front of the room until their names were called.

This time Alex was lucky. He got the first seat in the fourth row, right in the middle of the room. Allison was to the left of him and Peter Lesser to his right. Alex glanced at Peter as he put his books inside the desk. He looked like any other boy in the class, except that he wore glasses. Alex wondered how Peter felt, having to wear them every single day of his life!

Mrs. Miller seemed to know that her students needed time to get used to their new seats. Alex looked around. He noticed how different the room looked from before. The blackboard was closer. So was Mrs. Miller. She stood right in front of his desk as she said, "Now, class, take out your arithmetic books. We're going to work on problems."

Alex started off the lesson by paying attention. But then his mind began to travel, as usual. It traveled ahead to the rest of the day, picking out all the good parts. In half an hour he would be in gym. And then there was lunch and recess and the assembly. And after that, soccer practice. Not a bad day at all. If only he didn't have to worry about getting those darn glasses tomorrow. Which made him think about that awful spelling test he had taken before. He'd almost forgotten about the spelling test.

"Alex, what is the answer to the next problem?"

His head shot up like a jack-in-the-box. Mrs. Miller was standing at the back of the room. "Er—let me think a minute," Alex said. He didn't know which problem the class was working on, much less the answer.

"Are you paying attention, Alex?" Mrs. Miller asked.

"Yes, Mrs. Miller," Alex lied. He wished he knew what to say.

Alex thought he heard someone say "Forty" very softly, but he wasn't sure. He looked around. Both Allison and Peter had their eyes on their books.

"Looking around won't give you the answer," Mrs. Miller said from the back of the room.

"The answer is forty," someone whispered.

Alex smiled. This time he was sure he had heard.

"The answer is forty," he said loudly.

"Good, Alex. Laurie, please do the next problem."

Peter had given him the answer! Alex turned to the right and smiled. Peter gave a tiny nod.

Now why did Peter Lesser help him out of a tight spot like that?

5

Sorting It Out

Finally, after what seemed like hours, Mrs. Miller told the class to line up for gym. Alex was the first one out of his seat. He stood next to the open door and wished that Laurie and Allison would hurry. They always took their time because they didn't like gym.

How could someone not like gym? Of course, playing ball in gym class was not as exciting as his soccer games on Saturday. Still, it was great being on a team. And no matter where he was, Alex loved the feeling he got whenever he scored a point for his side.

Today they were playing kickball. It was Mrs. Miller's class against Mr. Fontaine's. And his amigo

Steve was in Mr. Fontaine's class. Alex leaned against the door. He didn't realize he was kicking until Mrs. Miller told him to stop.

"Hurry up, Laurie and Allison," he called to the girls. He couldn't wait for the kickball game to begin!

As usual, Mrs. Miller's class arrived first. Mr. Leoni, the gym teacher, told them to line up along one side of the gym and wait for Mr. Fontaine's class.

"They should be here any minute," he said.

Some kids laughed, but neither Mrs. Miller nor Mr. Leoni said anything. Finally the other class came.

"Hey, Amigo," Alex called out as soon as he saw Steve. But Steve didn't look at Alex.

That's funny, Alex thought. I sure yelled loud enough.

Mr. Leoni blew his whistle and told the children to quiet down. Alex *had* to call to his friend one more time.

"Hey, Amigo! Over here."

His voice rang out. No one else was talking.

"Alex Burman," Mr. Leoni said from the front of the gym. "Be quiet or I will have you stay after school."

Alex stared at his sneakers. A few girls were laughing. He *hated* being scolded in school, with everyone looking at him. And it was all Steve's fault for not greeting him back.

The kickball game started. Mrs. Miller's class was up. Alex was the fourth person to kick. He made a triple and brought in a run. His class cheered. Alex

felt good, but he still wondered: Why didn't Steve say hello to him when he came into the gym?

The teams changed sides. Alex was first baseman. He had to squint a lot to make sure he didn't miss the ball when he had to tag someone out at first base. Once Peter Lesser threw him the ball and Alex was able to tag the person out just in time. He had never noticed before, but Peter had a good arm. Not bad for someone who wore glasses.

Alex's class scored a few more times and was winning, six to three. Finally it was Steve's turn to kick the ball. He made a single. Now he *had* to speak to Alex.

Steve stood on first base and didn't look at Alex. He acted like Alex wasn't even there.

"Hey, Amigo," Alex said. "Why aren't you talking to me?"

"So I'm your amigo now? How come I wasn't yesterday?"

Alex looked at Steve. "I don't know what you're talking about."

Steve ran to second base. Alex shook his head. He couldn't figure out what was wrong.

At lunch Alex got in line to buy a sandwich and chocolate milk. He sat down at the table he always shared with Billy and Steve and some other boys. Two of the other boys, Johnnie and Ryan, were already eating their sandwiches.

"Hi, Alex," Ryan said. "Hurry up and eat, so we can get our game together."

"Sure thing," Alex answered, and bit into his sandwich. It was nice being wanted. But Ryan and Johnnie weren't as important to him as Billy and Steve. And Steve was mad at him.

Billy and Steve came into the cafeteria together. They were laughing.

"Hey, Amigo," Billy said, patting Alex's shoulder.

Alex made a circle with his hand. He couldn't talk because his mouth was full of his sandwich. Steve didn't say anything. What could he do to make Steve talk to him? Billy got in line to buy something to eat. Steve sat across from Alex and opened his lunch bag. He started eating his tuna-fish sandwich like everything was normal.

But everything wasn't normal.

"Are you going to tell me why you're mad at me?" Alex asked. He talked low. He didn't want Ryan and Johnnie, who were kidding around, to hear.

Steve stopped eating. He looked mad. "You know what's wrong. I mean, you're the one who wouldn't talk to *me*. And we're supposed to be amigos. Some amigo you are."

"What do you mean?" Alex asked. "When didn't I talk to you? I said hello to you twice in gym. And I got in trouble, too."

"That's today. But other days you act like you don't even know me. Like at your soccer game on Sunday. I mean, your game just happened to be near my aunt and uncle's, and I took my cousin to watch you play. But when I brought him over to meet you, you acted like you didn't know me. Your father noticed me before you did."

Alex could feel his cheeks growing warm. "Hey, Steve. Look, I'm sorry, okay? I just didn't—"

Steve reached across the table and grabbed Alex's arm to show he wasn't finished. "You did it again yesterday when our classes passed in the hall. I kept on waving, but you looked right through me. Like you didn't even see me."

"I did?" Alex asked. He remembered walking to the library with his class. Quietly, as Mrs. Miller had instructed. But he didn't remember seeing Steve.

"And then again, when the bell rang. I ran right by you and called out, but you pretended you didn't see me."

"It's so noisy in the halls at the end of the day," Alex said.

"But you acted like you didn't *see* me," Steve said.

I *didn't* see you, Alex thought. But he didn't dare say it aloud. Steve wouldn't mind that Alex was getting glasses. But if he told Steve, then Billy would find out. Billy would make fun of him, and that would be the end of Los Tres Amigos.

What could he say to show Steve that he didn't mean to hurt his feelings? "Steve, you know I'd never ignore you," Alex said. "Not on purpose. Sometimes my mind's a thousand miles away." He laughed. "Go and ask Mrs. Miller if you think I'm lying." Alex stuck out his hand. "Amigos?"

Slowly Steve put his hand across the table. "Yeah, why not? I just thought . . ."

Alex smiled. "Hey, we're Los Tres Amigos, aren't we? You and Billy are my best friends."

Alex shook his friend's hand hard. He was glad he'd cleared up the misunderstanding and Steve wasn't mad at him anymore. But Alex's smile was only skin-deep, as his grandma would say. Everything was getting complicated. Today he'd lied to both Billy and Steve, which made him feel squirmy inside. And he'd have to remember to squint more. He couldn't take the chance of not seeing Steve again in the halls.

Billy returned to the table, and Alex moved over to make room for him. Alex suddenly wasn't hungry anymore. He ate only half of his sandwich. He started kicking the back of his chair.

Darn it, having weak eyes was ruining his life. It was spoiling his good time with Steve and Billy. Alex squinted as he looked around the room. Maybe three kids in the entire cafeteria were wearing glasses. Why did *he* have to be like them instead of like Billy and Steve and all the other kids? Life wasn't fair. He kicked his chair harder.

Billy started to laugh. "Hey, guys, Alex is kicking. He's getting impatient to start our game."

One by one the others got ready to go outside. Alex smiled. May as well let them think that all he had on his mind was a ball game.

6

Four Eyes

Finally the five boys left the table. They threw their garbage in the open pail at the far end of the cafeteria. Then they ran toward the back door to the playground.

"Stop running, boys," Mrs. Harrington, a fifth-grade teacher, called to them. "You'll fall and hurt yourselves."

The boys slowed down. But outside they ran even faster.

" 'Stop running, boys,' " Billy imitated Mrs. Harrington. Alex, Steve, Ryan, and Johnnie laughed. Alex felt better. He was having fun with his friends. As soon as they rounded up some more kids, they could start their football game.

The sun was shining. It was warm for mid-October, and none of the boys wore jackets. Billy led them past the swings and the monkey bars to the open field. Kids, mostly girls, were swinging and climbing and chatting to each other. Alex squinted. A boy was on top of the monkey bars. It was Peter Lesser.

"Hey, Four Eyes," Billy called to Peter. "Be careful or you'll fall and break your glasses."

Steve and Ryan and Johnnie started laughing. Alex's ears turned red; he was embarrassed. It felt like Billy was making fun of *him*.

"Why do you always pick on him?" Alex asked Billy. "I mean, he doesn't bother you or anything."

Billy looked at Alex like he'd said something dumb. "Why not? Is Four Eyes suddenly a friend of yours or something?"

Alex looked down at the ground. "Well, he gave me an answer in math this morning."

Billy laughed. "Big deal. And why shouldn't he? He has enough brains for two people. Maybe three."

"But that doesn't mean you should call him names, does it? He can't help it if he needs glasses."

Billy stared at Alex. "It's a free country. Go and climb the monkey bars with Four Eyes if you want to. I won't stop you." He laughed and ran ahead.

Steve, Ryan, and Johnnie chased after Billy. Alex stood still for a minute, then he ran too. He felt awful. He didn't like the way Billy had treated Peter. He could only imagine what Billy would say when he found out that Alex was getting glasses too.

Alex walked slowly to the field where they always

played their ball games. Some other boys were there. Billy and Johnnie were starting to choose sides.

"I pick Alex," Billy said loudly. "Come here, Amigo. You're on my team."

Alex felt a little better because Billy chose him first. It proved Billy liked him after all—or did it? Maybe Billy chose Alex because he was one of the best athletes there.

Alex didn't know the reason, but it didn't make up for what Billy had said to him or to Peter.

7

Billy's Secret

Alex got to his classroom just as the bell rang. He was feeling happy again. He had scored a touchdown at the end of recess, and his team won the game. Alex was glad his class was going to an assembly. He had too many things on his mind to be able to think about schoolwork.

Mrs. Miller told the class to read a story for homework. Then she said, "We are going to the auditorium now. Please line up in two rows. Rows one and two together. Then three and four. Then five and six. And I expect you to walk next to your partner and keep two straight lines—not like some classes I can think of but won't mention."

Everyone laughed. They knew which class Mrs.

Miller was talking about. Besides always being late, Mr. Fontaine's class never walked in two straight lines.

Only Alex didn't laugh. He had to walk next to Peter Lesser. Alex felt funny walking next to Peter. Billy had just called Peter "Four Eyes." Peter knew that Alex was Billy's friend. And Alex always *used* to laugh when Billy called Peter "Four Eyes."

Some of the kids talked low as they walked to the assembly. They knew that Mrs. Miller wouldn't yell as long as they didn't make too much noise. Alex stared straight ahead so he wouldn't have to look at Peter.

They were halfway to the auditorium when Peter

said, "I saw you playing football. You're a real good quarterback."

"Thanks," Alex said. He felt good, the way he always did when someone complimented him. And he thought it was nice of Peter to compliment him. Especially after what Billy had called him.

"You're real good at math," he told Peter.

"I know," Peter said. "I'm going to be a mathematician."

Peter wasn't bragging, Alex realized. He was just stating a fact.

"Thanks for helping me out this morning," Alex said.

"That's okay."

Peter, Alex decided, was an all-right guy.

They were almost at the auditorium. Alex felt he had to say something about Billy.

"I'm sorry about Billy. What he said to you before."

Peter shrugged. "I never pay any attention to what comes out of Billy Harrison's mouth. You know why he's always going on like that—insulting everyone who crosses his path."

Alex's heart started to pound. "What do you mean?"

Peter gave Alex a look of surprise. "You know. Billy's acted like a bully ever since he was left back."

Alex was stunned! He shook his head to deny what Peter had just told him. Billy left back? Impossible! How could that be, when Billy was so smart? He always came up with the greatest ideas for Los Tres Amigos.

But maybe Peter was just saying that to get back at Billy for calling him names.

"You're making that up, aren't you?"

"Shh," Peter warned. Mrs. Miller was giving them the eye.

The class had to slow down because other classes ahead of them were entering the auditorium. Alex watched Mrs. Miller stop to talk to one of the other teachers.

"You're just saying Billy was left back because he calls you Four Eyes, right?" he asked again.

"Nope, it's true," Peter said. "We were both in Miss O'Brian's class in first grade. Only Billy was repeating the year. The whole class knew it too."

Alex was too stunned to speak.

"How come *you* didn't know? I thought Billy was your best friend."

"Yeah, but only since the summer. Billy and Steve went to the same day camp as I did. We were never in the same class."

Peter nodded. "So that's why you never knew."

Alex was about to continue when Mrs. Miller interrupted.

"Children, no talking now. Please follow me. Quickly," Mrs. Miller instructed. She led them to their seats at the front of the auditorium.

Alex hardly heard a word the woman on the stage was saying. Something about how important it was not to smoke or drink or take drugs. He was too busy trying to take what Peter had just told him and fit it in with everything he knew about Billy. Billy being left back was like looking into the sky and seeing two suns instead of one. It was crazy! Being left back meant a person was dumb. Only, Alex knew Billy was smart. The way a leader was smart. Alex shook his head. He was confused.

8

Soccer Practice

Alex walked slowly home from school. He was tired of squinting. And everything was different. Alex didn't feel like the same boy who had hurried to school that morning, eager for the day to begin.

He was sorry that he'd lied to Billy instead of telling him about the eye doctor. He was sorry that Steve had thought he was mad at him yesterday when the truth was Alex hadn't even *seen* Steve. That was the trouble, wasn't it? Alex thought. He couldn't see very well, but he didn't want anyone— not even his best friend Steve—to know. He didn't even like to admit it to himself.

Then there was the way Billy had spoken to him

when he'd tried to defend Peter. And that darn spelling test he probably failed!

But the thing that bothered him the most was what Peter had told him about Billy—that he had been left back. Of course, Billy wasn't dumb. So it probably meant he had some kind of learning problem that Alex knew nothing about.

Or maybe Peter was wrong.

But Alex knew in his heart that Peter was telling the truth. In a way it explained why Billy always said those things about people who were a little different. Calling out their weak points probably made Billy feel better than they were—or just as good.

It was hard to add this new information to what he knew about Billy and still see him as the leader of Los Tres Amigos.

Until today, Billy was the kid he had admired the most in the world.

Alex had a snack of milk and cookies. Then his mother drove him to soccer practice at a nearby elementary school. Alex's team, the Panthers, was made up of the best soccer players in the school district. The Panthers were a traveling team. They played against other traveling teams from nearby towns.

Alex was proud to be a Panther. Sometimes he wore his uniform when he was just watching television. His position was left wing. It was up to him and the other forwards to score lots of goals.

"Good-bye, Alex. I'll pick you up at five thirty," his mother said before she drove off.

"Thanks, Mom." Alex waved, then ran to join his teammates.

Soccer was Alex's favorite sport. He loved the moves of the game—using his feet and his head to advance the ball. He enjoyed the challenge of getting the ball past the other team's players and scoring a goal. And he was learning how important it was to pass the ball to another forward if the other player was in a better position to score.

Mr. Finkelstein, the coach, had the boys run around the field and do warm-up exercises. Then he divided the boys into two groups, A and B. Alex was on Team B.

"Okay, Panthers," he yelled. "We're going to have a practice game to get ready for the one on Saturday. Now the Tigers are real tough. They've won all three games so far, just like we have. If we beat them on Saturday, we'll be in first place in the league. Wouldn't that be great!"

"Yeah! Yeah!" the Panthers all shouted.

Alex raised his arms and shouted along with his

teammates. Mr. Finkelstein was always peppy and always encouraging the team to win. But he wasn't interested only in winning. He took the time to help each player improve. And he gave everyone, including the weaker players, playing time during games. Alex liked Mr. Finkelstein for that. He liked when people were fair.

The game began, and Team A got the ball. They dribbled it down the field toward Team B's goal. But Jimmy Rodriguez, who was playing fullback on Alex's side, booted it hard and sent it in the opposite direction. Alex grew excited as a player on Team B got the ball and started dribbling toward him. Soon it would be Alex's turn. And he would make a goal!

Alex squinted as the ball came closer. He went to meet it. But Jason Cole, who was playing center half on the opposing team, took it away. And Alex hadn't even seen Jason coming! Now how did that happen? Alex wondered.

Team A brought the ball back up their side, and this time they scored a goal. There was plenty of clapping and cheering. Alex was upset. They had

scored because he had lost the ball. And he had
been watching it so carefully, too. Well, it wouldn't
happen again.

Only it did. Almost the exact same way. He even
heard someone say, "Hey, what's with Alex?" Team
A cheered. Alex felt like crying.

Mr. Finkelstein called for ten minutes of rest. Alex walked slowly to where the other Panthers were sitting on the ground, drinking juice. Mr. Finkelstein tapped his shoulder.

"Come on," he said. "Let's talk."

9

Alex Decides

Mr. Finkelstein and Alex walked. When they were halfway across the field, Mr. Finkelstein asked, "What happened, Alex? Jason took the ball away from you twice. The same way, both times."

"I don't know," Alex murmured. "I was so sure I had the ball."

"Hmm," Mr. Finkelstein said. "It looked like you just didn't see what was happening around you."

"It did?" Alex felt sick. He remembered another time it had happened. The second game. The Panthers had almost lost because of him. Luckily, their center forward was able to get the ball again and score a goal.

Mr. Finkelstein stopped. He threw his arm over Alex's shoulders. "Maybe you need to wear glasses, Alex. It's not the worst thing in the world, you know."

They walked on. Alex didn't answer. He thought of the spelling test he'd probably flunked. And of hurting Steve's feelings.

"You'd be able to see everything clearly," Mr. Finkelstein said. "Without having to squint."

So Mr. Finkelstein noticed that he squinted. Maybe the whole world already knew that he needed glasses. Maybe that was why Mrs. Miller had had them change seats today—so Alex could sit closer to the blackboard.

"But I *hate* glasses!" Alex burst out. "Besides, how could I play soccer? They'd probably break and cut me or something."

"You know that's not true. Lots of professional athletes wear them. You'd wear safety glasses like they do, when you play sports."

Alex thought some more. "Glasses look so dumb," he finally said. "And they get in the way."

"We all manage," Mr. Finkelstein said, pointing to his sunglasses. "And you will too."

"Yeah, well, lots of people wear glasses, but it's different for kids," Alex said softly. "Other kids wise off."

Mr. Finkelstein patted his arm. "My left wing can handle that nonsense."

Alex nodded. He was beginning to think so too.

The next day at lunch, Billy was busy making plans while Alex and Steve finished their sandwiches.

"Hey, Amigos," he said. "Why don't we get up a football game after school? We can't play tomorrow, since Alex has a soccer game. And I have to visit my grandma on Sunday."

"Sounds good to me," Steve agreed. "We can start telling the kids about it during recess."

Billy looked at Alex. "All right with you?"

Alex cleared his throat. "Actually, I can't play this afternoon."

Billy smiled. "Do you have to go someplace with your mother again?" There was something in his voice that Alex didn't like. It made Alex nervous and angry at the same time.

"Right. I have to get glasses."

Billy stood up. He pointed a finger at Alex. "You! Glasses? You mean like Peter 'Four Eyes' Lesser?"

Alex looked at him for a minute. Then he said, "I'm nearsighted, so I need glasses. Other people have different problems. Like not doing so great in school."

Billy sat down. Steve looked at Billy, then at Alex. "Hey, Amigos. We're all friends, remember?"

Alex didn't say anything. He watched Billy. Billy looked like he was about to cry. That was something else Alex had to figure out—that maybe Billy wasn't as tough as he seemed to be. To Alex's surprise, this thought made him feel less angry with his friend. He wanted to show Billy that he cared about him— that his being left back didn't change anything where Los Tres Amigos were concerned.

"Hey, Amigos," Alex said. "Why are we wasting time sitting here? Let's play a game of football now." He sipped the last of his milk.

"Sure thing," Steve said. "Come on, Billy."

"Let's go, Billy," Alex said.

Billy looked at both of them and smiled. "Sure,

Amigos. We'll go get Ryan and Johnnie and the others."

· · ·

After lunch, Mrs. Miller's class had social studies. Laurie Doyle was reading aloud from the textbook.

"I'm getting glasses this afternoon," Alex whispered to Peter. The more times he said it, the easier the words came out of his mouth.

"You won't have to squint anymore," Peter said.

So Peter had noticed too!

"And you probably can get contact lenses when you're twelve. I'm going to."

"Yeah?" Alex had never thought about contact lenses before. "Do they hurt when you put them in?"

"Alex and Peter, stop talking," Mrs. Miller said. "I hope I'm not going to regret seating you next to each other."

Mrs. Miller didn't sound angry. In fact, when Alex squinted, he saw that she was trying not to smile.

Alex made himself concentrate on Ponce de León searching for the Fountain of Youth. But soon his mind started traveling. How could it not, when so much was happening? He'd learned to understand Billy a little better, and Peter was turning out to be a friend.

Wearing glasses wasn't going to be that bad. He no longer had to worry about Billy teasing him, and he'd see better when he played sports. He was sure to score lots more goals in soccer—maybe even get the Most Valuable Player award at the end of the season.

Alex smiled. Now, why hadn't he thought of that before?